W9-AXG-734

The Urbana Free Library

To renew: call 217-367-4057
or go to "urbanafreelibrary.org"
and select "Renew/Request Items"

Debt Dangers

By Paul Nourigat

If borrowing money is advertised as "easy", why not do it?

The truth is, taking out loans can create big problems for kids.

Debt Dangers is a great story about when loans
may be a good idea and when they're a risk.

Illustrated by Natalie Nourigat

FarBeyond Publishing LLC

Debt Dangers

A big thank you goes out to my wife and kids,
clients, co-workers, friends, parents, grandparents,
teachers, and librarians who chimed in on
this important topic.

The illustrations in this book were penciled by Natalie Nourigat,
inked by Emi Lennox, then digitally colored by Catherine Farris.

Text and Illustrations Copyright © 2012 Paul Nourigat
Manufactured in USA

FarBeyond Publishing LLC
ISBN 978-1-936872-03-9

Chelsea and Jack felt like they could not wait another second. For thirty minutes they had been anxiously standing by the front door with their dad, waiting to have a surprise celebration for their mom. Dad had told them, "Mom called to tell me about a promotion she got at work. She's very excited about it, and she wants to buy a new car with the extra money she'll earn at her new job."

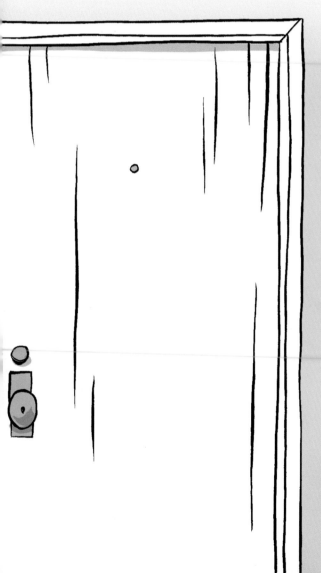

When they heard Mom's car door close outside, Chelsea and Jack wiggled with excitement, and Dad said, "Shhh. Here she comes."

"Surprise! Congratulations on your promotion!" they all shouted. Mom looked really surprised, and then her face broke into a huge smile. Dad hugged her and said, "Way to go! Getting a promotion is a great accomplishment. We know you worked hard to earn this."

Jack asked his mom, "What kind of car are you going to buy?" She said, "I don't know yet. I heard our bank is offering a good **loan** right now, and I need to talk to our banker to learn more about it. But for now, let's make a list of what we need and what we would like in a car. That way we'll be prepared to buy the car that's right for us." She smiled again. "I'm excited!"

Mom's car had been breaking down at inconvenient times. One day, she was late to work, and another time, Jack missed his guitar lesson because the car would not start. Both times, a tow truck took her car to a repair shop, which charged her a ton of money to fix it. A new car sounded like a great idea!

After dinner, while doing his chores, Jack asked Mom, "Why do you need a car **loan** from the bank when you'll make more money at your new job, and you and Dad have already saved money in your bank account?" His mom said, "Great question, Jack. We usually pay for things with money we have saved up, but cars can be very expensive. It can be hard to pay for something so large all at once. Also, the bank is advertising a really good **loan**."

Chelsea asked, "What makes a **loan** good?" Mom replied, "We can **borrow** money from the bank to buy the car now, and then pay the **loan** back over the next three years. Since I expect to drive the car for at least eight years, we'll not have to keep paying more money in years four through eight."

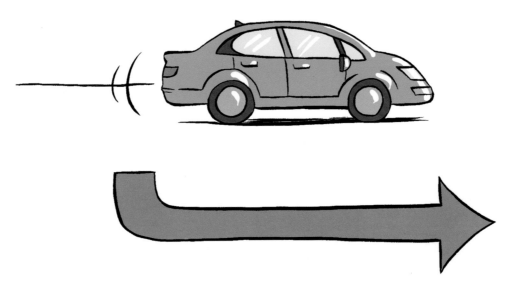

Jack was thrilled. "Why is the bank so nice to us?" he asked. Dad laughed. "Well," Mom explained, "When you **borrow** money, the bank charges you extra money, called '**interest**.' That is how they make the money they need to pay their employees and operate a special building that can protect our money.

We'll pay the bank a little extra each month—the **interest**—and we'll end up paying them back a little more than we **borrowed**. "

	Amount of Loan	$	32,000				
	Interest rate	7% per year					
Year		**Loan Balance**		**Loan Payments**		**Interest Fee**	
	$	32,000					
1	$	24,817	$	7,183	$	2,012	
2	$	17,115	$	7,702	$	1,493	
3	$	8,856	$	8,259	$	936	
4		0	$	8,856	$	339	
5		0		0		0	
6		0		0		0	
7		0		0		0	
8		0		0		0	
			$	32,000	$	4,781	$ 36,781

Total cost to buy car

"How will you pay the **loan** back?" asked Chelsea. Her mom explained, "Each month, we'll take some of the money from my paycheck, the money I earn from my job, and we'll send it to the bank as a **payment**. After making thirty-six **payments** over the next three years, we'll have paid the bank back."

Later, while Chelsea wiped off the table and Jack finished putting dishes away, their minds were racing. Suddenly, Jack set a cup on the counter with a loud clink.

"If we **borrowed** money from the bank too, we could buy tons of stuff that we aren't able to buy now. Think about it!" Chelsea considered what Jack had said, and replied robotically, "Clothes, toys, trips to cool places..." Jack added, "Parties, music movies, guitars, drums..."

"MOM AND DAD!" Chelsea and Jack yelled at the exact same time, running into the living room. Their parents looked startled when they ran in, but after the kids had explained their idea, Mom got that look that she always got when she was about to teach a lesson.

Mom said, "Each of you go get a pencil and paper, and let's meet at the dining room table."

A few moments later, Chelsea and Jack sat down. Mom helped them each make a list of all the things they wanted to buy, and then they estimated how much money it would take to get all the things on the list.

What we will buy with the money from our loan:		
	Chelsea	Jack
Clothes	$ 175	$ 75
Toys	$ 60	$ 125
Jewelry	$ 50	$ 0
Parties	$ 150	$ 75
Music	$ 50	$ 0
Drum set	$ 0	$ 450
	$ 485	$ 725

When they had each added up their totals, they said, "Wow, that is a lot of money!" at the same time.

Dad suggested, "Okay, now let's figure out how a **loan** would work for each of you." Using the computer, he showed the kids how much Chelsea's **payments** would be each month if she paid back the **loan** over 12 months. He also showed them the **interest** fee the bank would charge for a one year **loan**.

	Loan Payments	Interest Fee	Loan Balance
Amount of Chelsea's Loan	$ 485		
Interest rate	7%		
January	$39.14	$2.83	$445.86
February	$39.37	$2.60	$406.49
March	$39.60	$2.37	$366.89
April	$39.83	$2.14	$327.06
May	$40.06	$1.91	$287.00
June	$40.30	$1.67	$246.70
July	$40.53	$1.44	$206.17
August	$40.77	$1.20	$165.40
September	$41.01	$0.96	$124.39
October	$41.24	$0.73	$83.15
November	$41.48	$0.49	$41.67
December	$41.67	$0.24	$0.00
	$ 485	$ 19	$ 504

Total cost to buy stuff

Then Mom put on her really tough expression. She asked, "How will you pay back the **loan**?" Jack thought about it and replied, "The lemonade season is over because the weather has changed, so we won't make any money from our lemonade stand until next summer." Chelsea added, "Because school has started, there isn't much time left after homework and sports and music practice. I want to play with friends, not work at a job."

Nodding, Dad said, "If you cannot pay back money that you **owe**, then the **lender** can take things that you own, to sell them and get back some of their money. "Well," Chelsea said, frowning, "I wouldn't want to give up my toys or my clothes." Jack nodded his head nervously. Mom asked, "What about giving up your Red Flyer radio-controlled race car you earned from your summer lemonade stand?" "No way!" Jack and Chelsea said at the same time.

Jack said, "But the bank can earn a fee from **loaning** us money, so they'll want to give us a **loan**!" His mom replied, "Okay, but just imagine if someone wanted to **borrow** money from you, but they didn't have a job and probably couldn't pay you back anytime soon. Would you feel comfortable **loaning** them money?"
Chelsea and Jack both pondered Mom's question and Chelsea said, "No way!" while Jack said, "Probably not."

Looking at their list, Chelsea and Jack realized that those things would be fun to have, but not if they were unable to pay back their **loan**. Worse, because of the **interest** fee, everything would cost more than if they saved up their money and paid cash in the first place. Jack said, "I'm not sure I want a **loan** right now." Chelsea agreed, "It feels like we should save money and wait until we're older to get a **loan**."

Mom offered a great idea: "Why don't you come to the bank with me tomorrow after school? You can meet our banker while I apply for a car **loan**. You can show her your **loan** idea and see what she thinks. We can also ask her to tell us about **savings accounts**."

The kids agreed, and then Mom said it was time to get ready for bed. That night, Chelsea and Jack could hardly sleep, as they eagerly imagined meeting the banker! How much money do you think Chelsea and Jack should **borrow** from the bank?

The next day, Jack and Chelsea went with Mom to the bank, and Mom introduced them to her banker, Mrs. Capital. Mrs. Capital smiled and said, "Nice to meet you. Please sit down, and let's talk." She was very professional and polite, and Jack and Chelsea felt very important to be meeting with such an important person.

Mrs. Capital asked their mom lots of questions about her car **loan** and answered mom's questions about the **loan**. She also looked over some papers their mom had filled out.

Mrs. Capital entered some information into her computer, then looked up from the paperwork. With a big smile she told Mom, "Congratulations. Because of your job, your savings, and your history of paying your bills on time, we can offer you the **loan** you want for your new car." Mom looked really happy and Jack thought she was probably imagining the new car she would buy.

Then Mrs. Capital turned to Chelsea and Jack and asked, "And how may I help you today?" Jack explained, "We want a **loan,** like Mom's **loan**, but for less money. We want to buy smaller things, like toys and vacations. But we're unsure if a **loan** would be a good idea or not."

Mrs. Capital smiled and thanked Jack and Chelsea for coming in to talk to her, and Jack handed her the **loan** plan they had made at home. The banker reviewed their list and said, "Wow, you guys really did a nice job thinking things through. I am impressed with your planning." Chelsea said, "We're not sure a **loan** is a smart idea because we do not have jobs, and Mom says we should buy most things with money we already have, instead of **borrowing** and owing people money."

Mrs. Capital looked at Jack, who nodded in agreement. Then she studied the papers Chelsea and Jack had given her one more time before looking up with a big smile. "I think you have been wise, and I agree that a **loan** is not the right way to pay for these types of things, especially since you would struggle to pay it back."

Jack asked, "Why do companies on TV make **loans** sound so easy?" Mrs. Capital said, "Great question, Jack. The truth is that many companies will try to get you to **borrow** money or buy things from them even when it would not be the best thing for you to do. It's really important to only **borrow** money and buy things when you are really sure you can pay for them."

Jack looked at Mom. "We're very glad that you are getting a **loan** for your car." Nodding, Chelsea agreed, "Since you have a really good job, you can pay back the **loan**. And even if you or Dad lost your jobs, you could use the money in your special saving account to pay back the **loan**." Mom smiled and said, "Maybe someday, when you have more money in your **savings accounts**, you can think about getting a **loan** for something you need."

Mrs. Capital said, "Your mom mentioned on the phone that you are interested in opening **savings accounts**. Would you like to learn more about savings accounts today?" Excited, Chelsea and Jack quickly agreed.

Be a Saving Superstar!!!

Open an account today

✓ No fees

✓ Earn interest on deposits

✓ Free monthly statements

✓ Free online account access

Ask your banker to open an account for you

Start saving today

Handing them some shiny pamphlets, Mrs. Capital explained, "If you save money in an account at the bank, we'll pay you **interest** on the money you save." Jack said, "Seriously? You will pay us money if we keep money at the bank?" Chelsea exclaimed, "That is awesome!"

They agreed that it would be exciting to earn a little extra money and know that their money was safe at the bank and ready to use when they needed it in the future.

Mrs. Capital helped Jack and Chelsea fill out new account forms, which their mom also reviewed and signed.

How soon do you think they can start saving money in their **savings accounts**?

They decided to put that week's allowance into their new **savings accounts**. Mom said, "Your dad and I want to encourage you to save, and we'll add a dollar for every three dollars you save."

Mrs. Capital said, "That's great!" She handed them each a small red book. "Here is an account register, to help you keep track of the money in your account. From now on, whenever you deposit or withdraw money, write it down here, and then add or subtract to find out how much is in your account. That way, you will always know how much you have."

Date	Type	Description	Amount	Balance
November 1	Deposit	week's allowance	$3	$3
November 1	Deposit	mom and Dad help	$1	$4

Date	Type	Description	Amount	Balance

After they finished setting up their new **savings accounts,** Jack asked, "Can we see the bank vault?" Mrs. Capital agreed, and led Chelsea and Jack to the bank's **vault**, where money was safely stored. The **vault's** shiny steel door was huge and thick, with gigantic knobs and wheels.

Inside the **vault**, Mrs. Capital showed them hundreds of **safe-deposit boxes**. She explained, "People in the community use these to keep their valuables stored safely at the bank." "What do people put in the boxes?" asked Jack. Mrs. Capital said, "Our customers store everything from expensive jewelry to important financial paperwork and even precious pictures in their safe-deposit boxes."

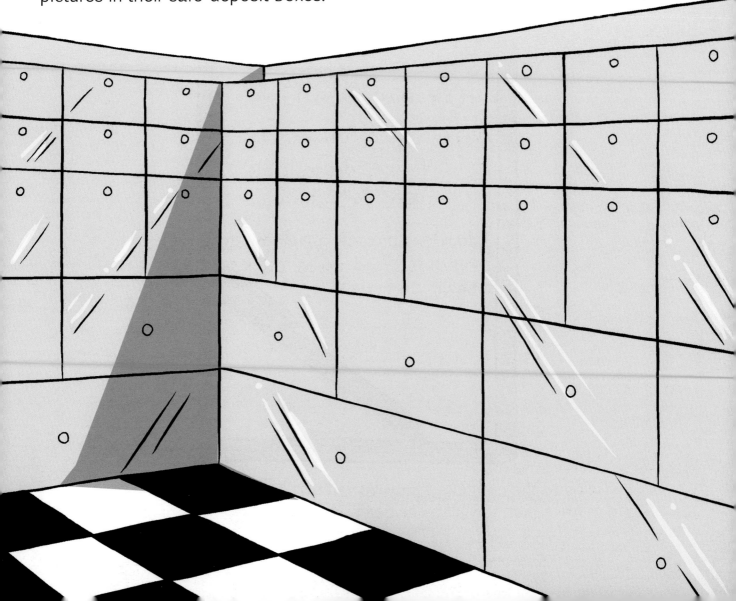

That night, the family sat down together and reviewed their list of "needs" and "wants" for Mom's new car. Dad thought the car should get good gas mileage, and Jack hoped it would be able to play music from Dad's portable music player. Chelsea wanted a sunroof. Mom mostly wanted a reliable car!

Our Car Wish List

Needs: good fuel mileage, 4 door, dependable, room for storage

Wants: sunroof, great music system, fold-down back seat, cool looking

Going to the computer, they researched prices and brands of cars, and made a plan to visit a car dealership that had good prices.

Finally, the big day came! Since she had made **loan** arrangements with the bank, Mom knew exactly how much she could spend and was prepared to buy a new car and drive it home. She still wanted the whole family to come along and look at the car, sit in it, ride in it, and help her be sure she picked the right one.

Looking around, Chelsea said, "It's amazing how many choices there are!"

What kind of car do you think they'll drive home?

Mom picked out a really cool car that had everything they needed, and most of the things they wanted. "I'm glad we don't **owe** anybody money," Jack said to Chelsea. "Yeah, I'm glad we're earning **interest** in our **savings accounts** instead of *paying* **interest** for a **loan**," Chelsea agreed.

They were both quite happy that their mom and dad had made a good loan decision and could drive them home in a super-cool car!

Financial Glossary

Not sure what that word meant? Below are some important words and concepts used in this book and their definitions:

Borrow ... To take something from someone, with an agreement you will give it back sometime in the future.

Interest ... Extra money that a borrower pays to a lender in exchange for borrowing money.

Interest rate ... The way that interest cost is calculated.

Lender ... A person or company who lends money.

Loan ... Something you receive, which must be returned or paid back.

Owe ... To have a responsibility to pay something back.

Payment ... How much of a loan you pay back at one time, each month, for example.

Safe-deposit box ... A place at the bank where people can store and protect things they care about.

Savings account ... A type of bank account that pays people interest on the money they keep in the account. To save is to set aside money.

Spent ... When money is gone because it was used to buy something.

Vault ... A strong and safe place inside a bank where money and other valuables are stored.

Tips for Kids
Things to remember about borrowing

It's best to buy things only when you can pay for them.
> Even if you think you may have more money later, you can never be sure. So it makes sense to wait to buy things until you can afford something rather than borrow.

You should only borrow money when you are sure you can pay back the lender.
> If you cannot pay back a **loan**, your *savings* and other things you care about can be taken from you, and other people will not want to loan you money in the future.

Don't borrow money unless the terms of the loan—such as when it must be paid back and the interest rate—are good for you.
> A loan with bad terms can make it hard for you to pay back the money, costing you more money than a good loan.

Ask your parents
> It is always smart to discuss money with your parents before you decide if an idea about money is a good one. Sometimes just talking about it will help you make a good decision.

Learn more about saving money at www.MarvelsOfMoney.org

Tips for Parents
Important concepts about borrowing

Encourage your children to "live within their means."
>   This will help them avoid consumer debt and lifestyle decisions that may result in their having to play catch-up for the rest of their lives.

Share your decision-making processes with them.
>   Provide a real-world view of lending by reviewing one of your loans with your children and showing them the payments you make, as well as the total cost of the loan, including fees and interest charges.

Teach your children to shop wisely.
>   Involve your children in a buying decision and take extra time to review the cost of borrowing that the lender is required to disclose, compared to a cash purchase. Show them how smart buying decisions, balanced with delayed gratification will reduce the need to borrow.

Bring them along for the ride.
>   Take your children to your financial institution, outlining beforehand what your purpose is. Discuss the visit after it's completed. Periodically introduce your children to business and financial professionals in order to make such practices comfortable and natural.

Find great resources and tools at www.MarvelsOfMoney.org

About the author

Paul Nourigat has advised families, businesses, and community leaders across the country for over 28 years.

In addition to his time spent with thousands of highly successful people, he has invested extensive time with families who are struggling with money. As a result, Paul developed a clear understanding of "what works" and "what doesn't" in business and personal finance.

Having heard over and over "I wish I had learned more about money when I was young", he set out on a mission to teach young people about money using a very unique approach. Blending extensive graphics and fictional stories which young people connect with, Paul is breaking new ground by using the graphic novel format to teach financial literacy.

About the illustrator

Natalie Nourigat is a recent college graduate enjoying financial independence

and her career as a freelance artist. At 16, she created her first website, where she began publishing and selling her artwork.

She enjoys earning a living doing what she loves, in the vibrant community of artists in Portland, Oregon.

Natalie's many other works can be found at natalienourigat.com

Books from the author

"Why is there Money?" (For younger readers, ages 5-8 years)
This poetic journey through history shows the path from bartering to currencies, to credit, to the modern financial tools used by adults. Kids will enjoy the beautiful original images as they visualize the fascinating evolution of world commerce.

"Marvels of Money ... for kids" (For young readers 7-12 years)
Richly illustrated, engaging and practical stories for young readers about the fundamentals of money. Five stories follow Chelsea and Jack through life experiences which kids will recognize, while showing how they deal with financial struggles, decisions and actions. 200 pages of engaging original illustrations, fictional stories, glossaries for new vocabulary and even a "Tips for Parents" section!

"Earning Excitement", "Spending Success", "Debt Dangers", "Giving Greatness", and "Terrific Tools for Money" are available as separate books or combined in a 5 story book.

"If Money Could Shout: the brutal truths for teens" (For readers 13-19 years)
A breakthrough graphic novel for teens and young adults about money and the choices which will affect their lives in a big way. Eight fictional stories illustrated by eight talented artists from diverse parts of the United States. Over 400 vivid illustrations compliment the eight captivating stories about the lives of teens and how they deal with financial decisions. Visually stunning, deep in messaging, highly engaging for young people who would love an alternative to a "text book" on the topic of personal finance and life success.